Book Two

Written By Brett Gunning & Stacy Padula

Illustrated by Maddy Moore

Copyright © 2021 Brett Gunning and Stacy Padula.
All rights reserved.

This is a work of fiction. Names, characters, places, and incidents are either a product of the author's imagination or are used fictitiously, and any resemblance to actual persons, living or dead, business establishments, events, or locales is entirely coincidental. No part of this book may be reproduced or transmitted in any form or by any means, graphic, electronic, or mechanical, including photocopying recording, or taping without the written consent of the author or publisher.

Briley & Baxter Publications | Plymouth, Massachusetts

ISBN: 978-1-954819-27-6

Book Design: Stacy O'Halloran

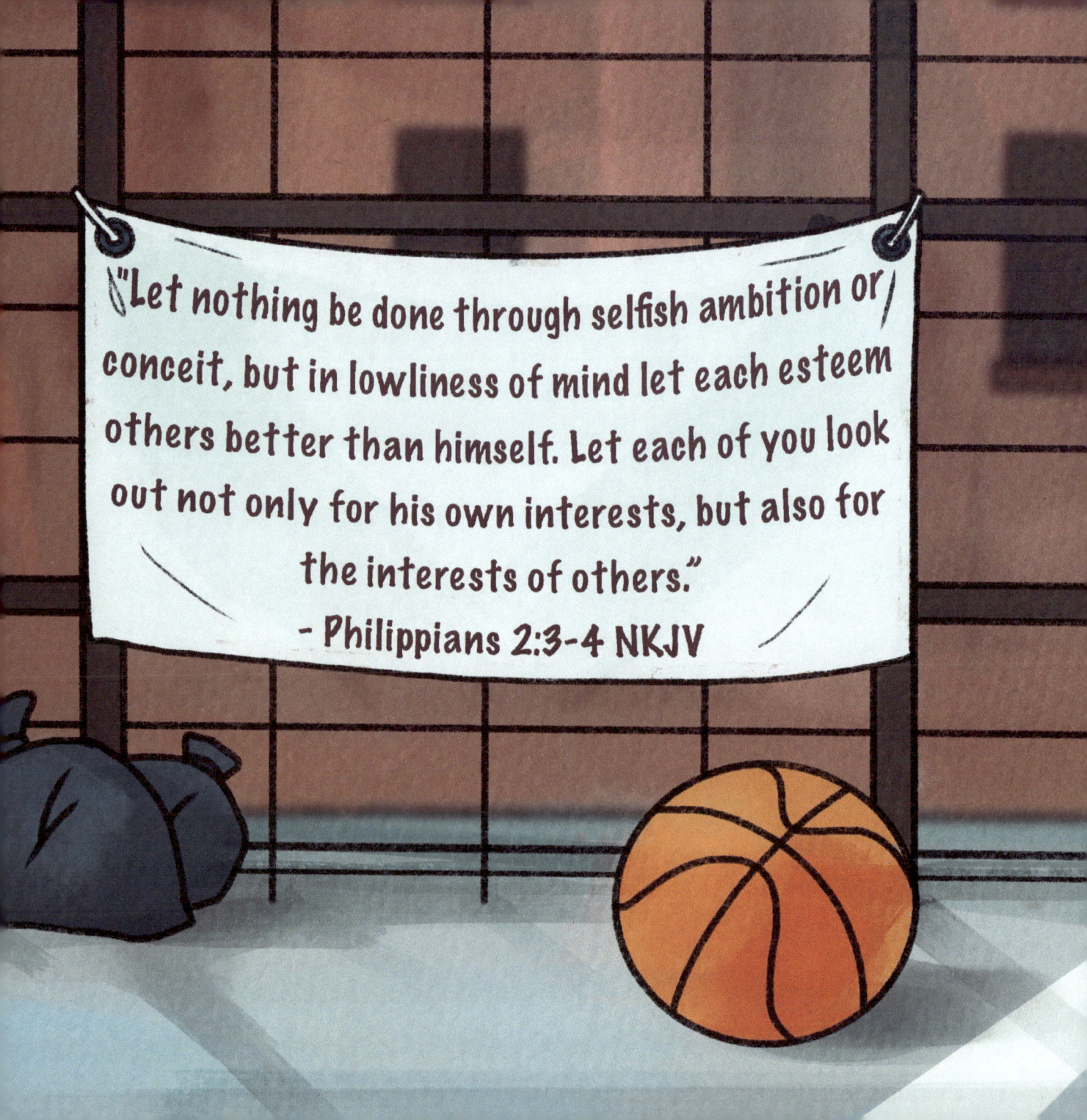

About On The Right Path

On the Right Path (OTRP) is a non-profit organization founded in 2020 by current NBA Assistant Coach Brett Gunning. The mission of OTRP is to guide youth basketball players on the right path to achieving their maximum potential through education, mentorship, and skill development. OTRP also provides parents and coaches with tools and resources to effectively keep their child or player on the right path. The core principles are guidance, inspiration, and creativity and offer 12 basketball skill pillars and 12 life skill pillars. Gunning's inspiration comes from his 26 years of coaching in college and in the NBA.

About Brett Gunning

Brett Gunning has spent the last 26 years coaching in college and in the NBA. He began his career in 1994 as an assistant coach for Jay Wright at Hofstra University. Over the next seven seasons, he was a part of a staff that turned Hofstra into an American East powerhouse, posting a 72-22 (.766) record from 1998-2001. He was very instrumental in the development of the Pride players, and he assisted with recruiting, scouting and film analysis.

He then went on to spend seven seasons (2001-08) as a member of the coaching staff at Villanova University, again working under the leadership of Head Coach Jay Wright. During his time with the Wildcats, Gunning played a vital role in recruiting and developing a unit that secured four straight NCAA Tournament berths and made three trips to the Sweet 16. He was named associate coach in 2005 and was recognized following the 2007-08 season as one of the top 25 assistants in the nation by Rivals.com. Gunning's responsibilities with Villanova included on-court teaching, recruiting and scouting.

Gunning's NBA career began when he joined the Houston Rockets in 2008 as the team's director of player development. In that role, he was responsible for improving player performance through on-court, one-on-one skill development and the use of video analysis. He was later named an assistant coach for the Rockets prior to the 2011-2012 season before leaving to serve in that same role with the Orlando Magic for 3 seasons from 2012-2013 through 2014-2015. He then returned to the Rockets as an assistant coach in 2015, and from 2016-2020, he assisted Head Coach Mike D'Antoni coordinate the Rockets offensive scheme. During the 2017-2018 season, the Rockets won a franchise record 65 games and advanced to the Western Conference Finals.

About Stacy Padula

Author and entrepreneur, Stacy A. Padula from Plymouth, Massachusetts has accrued years of experience working with adolescents as a college counselor, mentor, life coach, and youth group leader. In 2019 and 2020 respectively, the International Association of Top Professionals (New York, NY) named her "Top Educational Consultant of the Year" and "Empowered Woman of the Year." She is the CEO and founder of both South Shore College Consulting & Tutoring and Briley & Baxter Publications—a publishing company that donates a portion of its proceeds to animal rescues each month. She is the author of the Gripped and the Montgomery Lake High young-adult book series. Her first novel, The Right Person, was published in 2010, followed by When Darkness Tries to Hide, The Aftermath, The Battle for Innocence, and The Forces Within. Throughout 2019 and 2020, she released a new series titled Gripped, which takes place in the same world as Montgomery Lake High but focuses on different main characters. Multiple Gripped books became #1 New Releases in their genre on Amazon. In 2019, she also wrote her first screenplay, an adaptation of her novel The Aftermath and worked on a pilot script for Gripped, which has been embraced by Hollywood producers. Learn more at www.stacyapadula.com.

About Maddy Moore

Sylvia Madison (Maddy) Moore is a recent graduate from the University of Pennsylvania who completed her Bachelor of Arts degree in Archaeology and Fine Arts. Moore grew up in a family of international coaches and has consequently lived and worked in various corners of the world, including Singapore, New Zealand, and throughout Europe. She began her career as an artist at fifteen, where she would complete commission-based illustrations for clients around her school commitments. In recent years, Moore has worked full-time as a freelance artist with authors and designers from around the art world to bring their projects into fruition, including but not limited to comic book illustrations, character designs, cards and flyers, logos, and her personal work on the indie webcomic, "The Cloud Maker." Moore currently resides in Delaware County, Pennsylvania, just outside of Philadelphia.

CPSIA information can be obtained
at www.ICGtesting.com
Printed in the USA
LVHW072111240921
698701LV00002B/4